A Biff Bam Booza Publication
Rocket Red: A Little Ant with a Big Dream © Copyright 2021
Waterhole Productions, LLC

Publisher's Cataloging-in-Publication data

Names: DaVeiga, Cheryl, author. | Gibson, Dave, author. | Ram, Remesh, illustrator.
Title: Rocket red : a little ant with a big dream / written by Cheryl DaVeiga; illustrated by Remesh Ram.
Description: Nashville, TN; Waterhole Productions, LLC, 2021. | Summary: Rocket Red is a small ant with a big dream and a big problem. This is a fun-filled and pun-filled adventure that focuses on determination, friendship, and the power of music.

Identifiers: ISBN: 978-1-7363951-5-8 (hardcover) | 978-1-7363951-4-1 (paperback) | 978-1-7363951-6-5 (ebook)
Subjects: LCSH Ants--Juvenile fiction. | Music--Juvenile fiction. | Friendship--Juvenile fiction. | BISAC JUVENILE FICTION / Animals / Insects, Spiders, etc. | JUVENILE FICTION / Action & Adventure / Survival Stories
Classification: LCC PZ7.1.D33688 Roc 2021 | DDC [E]--dc23

Hi, I'm Frank TL Frogg.
The TL stands for "The Lucky"
and that's Frogg with an extra g.

I'm the croaking spokesman for my online
home, BiffBamBooza.com, where my puppet
friends and I share adventures in books,
sing-along videos, and multimedia flipbooks.

The star of this Biff Bam Booza adventure
is my friend, Rocket Red. He's a rock star,
and you're never going to believe that . . .
he's an ant!

As you read about Red's fantastic journey,
count all the ants hidden in the story.
Then, go to BiffBamBooza.com to see
if you found them all.

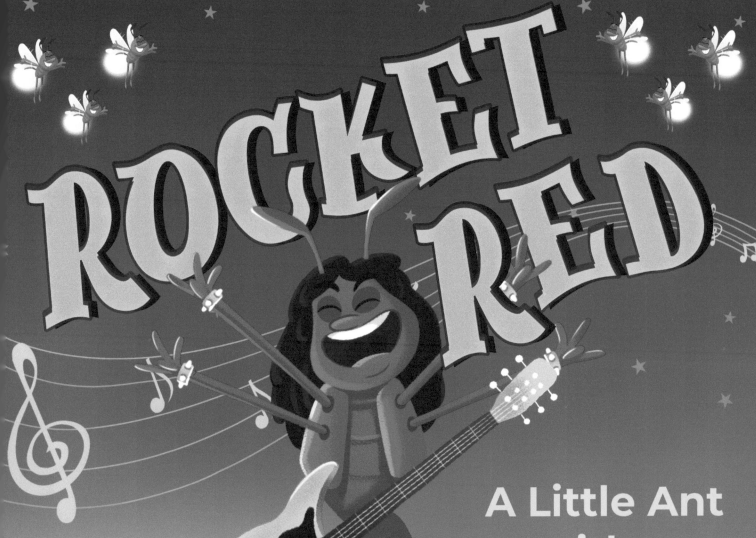

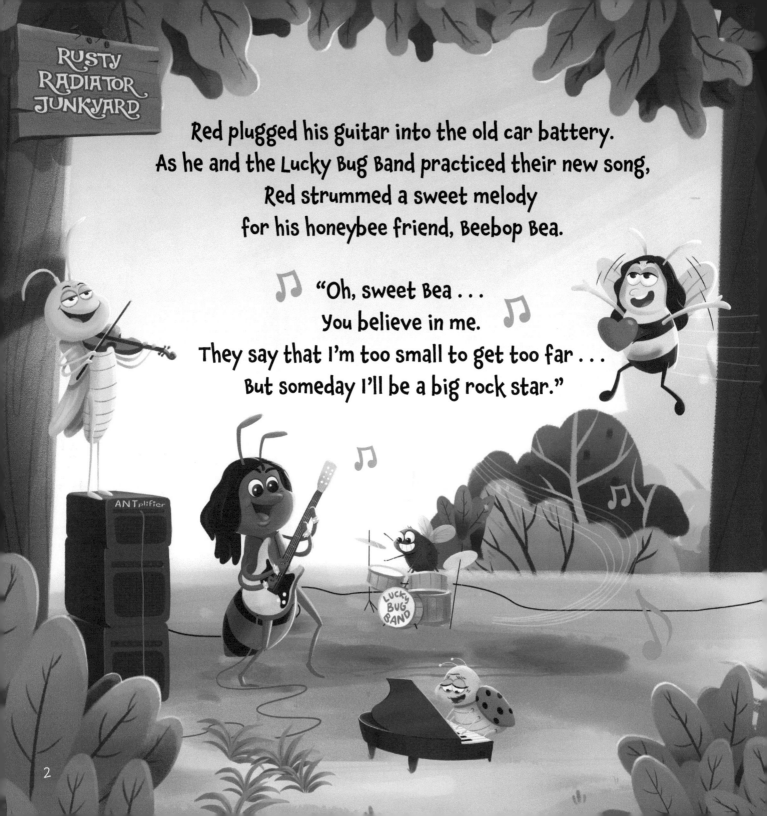

Red plugged his guitar into the old car battery.
As he and the Lucky Bug Band practiced their new song,
Red strummed a sweet melody
for his honeybee friend, Beebop Bea.

"Oh, sweet Bea . . .
You believe in me.
They say that I'm too small to get too far . . .
But someday I'll be a big rock star."

Beebop Bea swayed to the music
and did a little waggle dance.
Red's music always made her feel
instantly joyful.

3

Suddenly Red's mom Queenie
flew in from Colony Anthill.

4

"Red! Stop all those antics!
Put down that guitar!" Queenie snapped.
"Get to the picnic ground and help the workers bring up our meal.
Someone left a delicious whopper of a burger,
and we need every set of legs we have
to muscle that burger up the hill!"

5

In a flash, the band scattered.
Bea made a beeline for the exit.

Red looked away. His plans did *not* include scouting around
for someone's leftover lunch and dragging it up a hill.
Red had fantasies of making it big, like his heroes, the Beetles.

6

"Mom, can't you see how music feeds my heart and soul?" Red pleaded.

"Your music won't feed the colony," Queenie scoffed. She raised her antennae. "Redmond Anthony . . . GO!"

"I'm going," Red said, as he trudged toward the picnic ground.

"Over here, Red!" the ants called from the burger.
It DID smell yummy.

But before Red reached his friends,
a huge dark shadow passed over him, missing him by an inch.

"Yikes!" Red gasped.

The dark shadow came again. Red realized it was attached to . . .
a giant black shoe! He was about to be *squished!*

The shoe came down,
down, down . . .

"Oh no, oh no,
oh no!"

9

In his biggest voice,
the one he used for wailing out rock and roll songs,
Red shouted, "WAIT! PLEASE!"

The shadow moved away—just in time.

"Did I hear something?"
the big, mean-looking man who belonged
to the shoe muttered.
"Nope, there's nothing here but a pesky little ant."

10

"Ants aren't welcome at picnics!"
Mr. Big and Mean bellowed.
He raised his shoe again.

But just then,
Mr. Big and Mean
noticed something shiny
on Red's back,
and he stopped.

Red had to think fast.
He began to play louder than ever.
It sounded merely like a distant hum
to Mr. Big and Mean.

Red saw the huge face coming closer
. . . and closer.

Red wailed out an old Beetles song:

"HELP! Can't you hear me? HELP!!"

13

"Well I'll be an ant's uncle!"
the big voice boomed. "What have we here?"

"Please!" begged Red.
"If you don't step on me,
I'll . . . I'll . . . I'll rock your picnic.
Free antertainment!"

Mr. Big and Mean chuckled.
He scooped Red up with a butter knife
and placed him on top of his shoe.
The seconds ticked by . . . tick . . . tock.
To Red, it felt like hours.

Finally, Mr. Big and Mean spoke.
"Well, I guess we *could* use a little music.
Hey, gang, come on over!"

Red strummed and plucked and wailed.
He sang for his life, loudly crooning:
"Give ants a chance, man!"

But Red's little guitar and voice
weren't loud enough for Mr. Big and Mean
or the others to hear,
and he didn't have his antplifier.
He was too small!
People began to walk away.
No!

Then suddenly, Red saw thousands of ants—and uncles—
from Colony Anthill marching to help him.
They brought the fiddling grasshopper
and the whole Lucky Bug Band. They even brought the Beetles!
Together, they dragged the big, heavy antplifier.

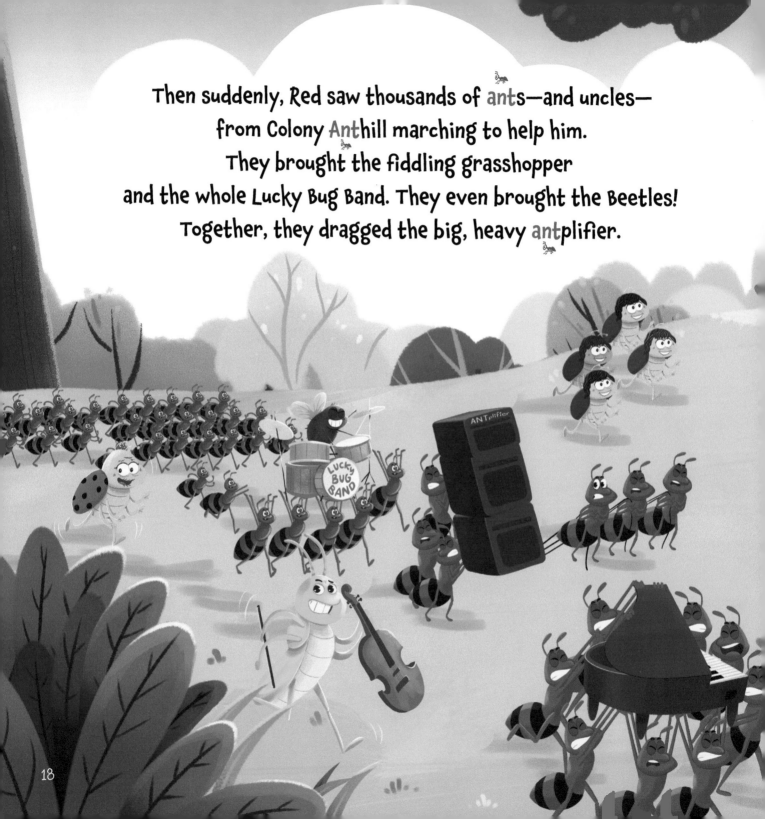

"Wow! You DO believe in me," Red said.
"But the antplifier won't work
without the battery from the junkyard car!"
He sighed.

Then, to Red's glee, in flew Bea
with a bee-powered battery pack strapped to her back.
Her friends from the hive swarmed behind her.
Together, they whizzed and buzzed and flapped their wings,
making Bea's battery pack hum with power.

It worked!
Red's guitar came alive.
The Lucky Bug Band joined in.

21

The sound got loud . . . and louder . . . and LOUDER,
and the people heard it!
They clapped their hands and roared, "FANTASTIC!"

They shouted, "Rock it, Red! Rock it, Red!"

And the chant became his new name, ROCKET RED!

The people danced and sang and hooted and hollered until dark.
"Give us an encore, Rocket Red!" they yelled.

Fireflies lit up the sky while Red played his new anthem,

"Don't Raid on My Parade."

The music brought them all together—
big and small, bugs and beasts, and people of all shapes and colors.
Red and the Lucky Bug Band
took a bow on on the big black shoe.
Queenie beamed with pride.

24

Now the townsfolk invite the ants
to share in every picnic.
This is what Red always wanted—
to play his guitar and make music.

His dream finally came true.

How many ants did you count?
Go to BiffBamBooza.com to see if you found them all.

Let Frank TL Frogg bug you with some fun facts:

- Honeybees really do what's called a *waggle dance*, as Beebop Bea did, to let their hive mates know when they've found some nectar.

- Ants are strong. They can lift 20 times their own body weight, so carrying a burger up the hill would be an easy task.

- Queen ants have wings and can fly, just like Queenie flew in from her colony.

- Ants don't have ears, but they can feel musical vibrations, like the ones from the Lucky Bug Band, through their feet on the ground.

- Rocket Red was inspired by a real guitarist named Ant. In nature, worker ants are female, so Red would have been a girl in real life. Rock on, girls!

We hope you enjoyed this Biff Bam Booza publication.

Biff Bam Booza is an interactive platform of trusted entertainment for kids!
Featuring books, sing-along videos and multimedia flipbooks
with quirky characters and puppets,
it's a fun place to learn to be your very best YOU
and laugh out loud as you build reading and life skills.

Go to BiffBamBooza.com where you can:

- Meet Frank TL Frogg and his puppet friends
- Sing along with Rocket Red to his song for Beebop Bea
- Find other Biff Bam Booza books and multimedia flipbooks and sing-along videos
- Join the Biff Bam Booza Kids Club and get lots of goodies

See you there!

CPSIA information can be obtained
at www.ICGtesting.com
Printed in the USA
BVHW021648101221
622097BV00001B/1